F Robinson
Robinson, Nancy K.
Just plain cat

W9-AQO-573

NOV 1981
RECEIVED
OHIO DOMINICAN
COLLEGE LIBRARY
COLUMBUS OHIO

Just Plain Cat

by Nancy K. Robinson

SCHOLASTIC BOOK SERVICES
NEW YORK · TORONTO · LONDON · AUCKLAND · SYDNEY · TOKYO

J
R

With thanks to Barbara Linton and David Eisendrath...

No part of this publication may be reproduced in whole or in part, or stored in a re-
trieval system, or transmitted in any form or by any means, electronic, mechanical, photo-
copying, recording, or otherwise, without written permission of the publisher. For information regarding permission, write to Scholastic Book Services, 50 West 44 Street, New
York, N.Y. 10036.

0-590-31782-2

Text copyright © 1981 by Nancy K. Robinson.
All rights reserved. Published by Scholastic Book Services, a division of
Scholastic Magazines, Inc.

12 11 10 9 8 7 6 5 4 3 2 1   1   1 2 3 4 5 6/8
Printed in the U.S.A.   01

This book is dedicated
to
Beatrice Schenk de Regniers.

115168

Unfair

Chris woke up. Today was the first day of school. He was starting the third grade. And he was in a terrible mood.

When he went to get dressed, he remembered that he had nothing new to wear—not even a new T-shirt.

"You don't need a thing this year," his mother had said cheerfully. "Everything still fits."

That made Chris miserable. If everything still fit, even his pants, he hadn't grown much over the summer. That meant that every girl in the class would still be taller than Chris. He saw himself surrounded by giant girls. It was like a nightmare. "Maybe some of them got a little shorter over the summer," he thought. No, that never happened. That was too much to hope for.

His feet hadn't even grown. He could still wear the same worn-out sneakers. That had really made his mother happy.

"Thank goodness they fit," his mother had said. "We're a little short of money right now."

Chris's father was a photographer. He worked very hard, but he didn't always get paid on time. Chris often heard his father complain about all the rich people who owed him money for photographs. It made Chris angry to think that some big-shot businessman owed his father a bunch of money and Chris was the one who had to suffer. It was so unfair!

But sometimes Chris got angry at his father, too. Why couldn't his father have an ordinary job in an office—the kind where you brought home money every week. Then they would be able to go away on a summer vacation like everyone else. Then his parents would stop having those boring discussions about rent, food prices, and electric bills.

Chris didn't even get a new book bag this year. He would have to carry the same old beat-up blue bag with his last year's notebook in it. And he would have to use an old chewed-up pencil that his mother had found. The eraser on it was OK and, "It writes just the same," his mother had said, but Chris decided he would do his best to lose it the first day.

"It's not fair," Chris whispered over and over. "It's just not fair." He looked in the mirror to see how sad and miserable he looked, but he just looked sulky. That was no good. Chris spent the next few minutes in front of the mirror. He could hear his mother in the kitchen.

Finally he was satisfied with the expression on his face. A little sad, but not angry. Helpless. A pitiful short kid. That would make his mother feel bad. Now he just had to hold that expression until he got to the kitchen.

When Chris passed the living room, he heard snoring. He peeked in the door. There was his father fast asleep on the couch. His father was wearing the same clothes he had worn the day before. Chris felt bad. He knew his father had been working late into the night, printing photographs. His father had his own darkroom for printing photographs right behind the kitchen. He never had to send rolls of film to the camera store; he did it all at home. But all weekend he had been so busy in that darkroom, he had had no time for Chris.

Chris suddenly realized he might be late for school. He didn't have time to go back to the mirror and get that pitiful expression back on his face, so he tiptoed past the living room, down the hall, and into the kitchen.

The kitchen was a mess. There were brown bottles of chemicals all over the place. His father's print dryer was sitting on the breakfast table, and Chris could hear the water running in the darkroom. That meant there were more photographs being washed. The job wasn't finished yet.

His mother looked tired. Chris was sure she had been up all night, helping his father dry photographs. She looked at Chris as if she were surprised to see him.

"Hi, dear," she said. Then she tried to clear a little space on the table. She put down a bowl and began pouring cereal into it.

"Isn't there something else?" Chris asked. "I don't like that cereal."

His mother stopped pouring cereal. For a moment she looked as if she were going to cry. "Well, you certainly woke up on the wrong side of the bed."

Chris sat down and quietly ate his least

favorite cereal. His mother poured herself a cup of coffee and sat down across from Chris. She sighed.

"I'm sorry, Chris. I can't cook anything with these chemicals around. I'll make you waffles tomorrow."

"Doesn't matter," said Chris. But it did matter. Wasn't there anything special about today? Shouldn't he be treated differently? After all, he was a third grader for the first time in his whole life.

His mother looked at the clock and jumped up. She opened the print dryer and carefully took out a photograph. It was a photograph of the inside of a factory. There were bottles lined up as far as the eye could see. It was a beautiful photograph, Chris thought.

His mother went into the darkroom and came back carrying another wet photograph. She put it on a shiny metal sheet, like a cookie sheet.

"Mom." Chris knew this wasn't the right time to ask, but he couldn't help it. His mother was trying to get the extra water off the photo with a rubber tool called a *squeegie*.

"Mom," he said again. "When Orpex pays Daddy, could we get a kitten?"

"Oh, Christopher." His mother turned the photo over and began wiping the water off the other side. "You know it's not just the money. There are fifty different reasons why we can't have a cat."

"Fifty?" Chris was shocked. Yesterday there had only been four reasons, and he was ready with the answers to all four. Today there were fifty! Chris subtracted in his head. How could he come up with the answers to forty-six more?

His mother laid the damp photo on the dryer and pulled a cloth tightly over it. She looked at the clock. Chris waited. He wanted her full attention.

When she sat down and sipped her coffee, Chris began:

"Look, Mommy, I've got it all figured out. You see, it won't cost you hardly anything. We'll get the kitten at the Bide-a-Wee home. That's seven dollars and a little more for shots. I'll pay my whole allowance for cat food plus the money I get from Mrs. Hawkins for errands. We can have its claws taken out like Veronica's cat so it won't scratch the furniture." (Veronica lived across the hall; she had a dog *and* a cat. It was so unfair!)

Chris took a deep breath and went on, "I'll feed it and change the litter so there won't be any work for you and . . ."

Chris stopped. His mind went blank. He had the feeling he had answered only three of the four reasons. He counted quickly to himself: "One—too expensive. Two—scratching the furniture. Three—too much work." What was the fourth reason? He knew he had an answer to that one too.

"The main thing," his mother said slowly, "is your father's darkroom. We can't have cat hairs around. It would ruin his negatives."

"I'll keep him out!" Chris shouted. "I'll make a gate—a special gate so he can't get through. Oh, please, Mommy, please . . ."

His mother stood up. She came over to hug Chris. Chris pulled away from her—even though he didn't mean to.

"We'll talk about it later," his mother whispered. "Hurry now, you'll be late." She handed him his lunch box.

Chris forgot everything when he saw that lunch box. It was his second-grade lunch box and it had a picture of some rabbits dressed in bathing suits having a picnic. In second grade,

Chris had thought it was a pretty nice lunch box, but he couldn't bring a lunch box like that to third grade.

"Oh, Mom, couldn't I bring my lunch in a paper bag?" (Fifth graders always brought their lunches in paper bags.)

"Don't be silly," his mother said. "That gets too expensive."

Veronica

Chris waited in the hallway for the elevator. He tried to hide his lunch box behind his back. He hoped he wouldn't bump into Veronica.

Veronica had been in his class last year, but she was going to a different school this year. She was going to a private school. Her school didn't start for another week.

The elevator door opened. Chris got in. There were already a few people in it.

Before the door could close again, everyone heard a shriek. "Hey, hold the elevator! Hold the elevator!"

Chris didn't want to, but he pushed the OPEN button. A small white poodle tugging at its leash came rushing in. Right behind the dog was Veronica, who was still yelling.

"Let us in! Let us in! Lady Jane Grey has to go to the bathroom."

The people in the elevator moved aside for Veronica. They made even more room for the small white poodle.

Chris looked down at the poodle. The little dog was sitting politely and patiently with her head cocked to one side. Lady Jane Grey was busy looking at everyone's shoes; she didn't act as if *she* were the one in a hurry.

But Veronica was tapping her foot impatiently. Every time the elevator stopped, she moaned, "Oh, no-o-," and looked crossly at the people who got in. She gave Mrs. Hawkins a particularly cross look.

"Hurry up, hurry up," she muttered.

Chris tried to move away from Veronica. It was not just because she was being so rude; he didn't want anyone to notice that Veronica was taller than he was. Veronica had grown a lot during the summer. She had also put on weight. Her shiny brown hair was very long now, and she wore it tucked back behind her ears. She looked very grown up. Chris felt like a baby when he stood next to her.

"Hello, Chris." Mrs. Hawkins smiled at him. "First day of school?"

Chris nodded shyly. He liked Mrs. Hawkins. She was very old and walked with a cane. It was hard for her to get out of her apartment. Chris often did errands for her, and she paid him ten cents an errand. ("She's ripping you off," Veronica once told him.)

Mrs. Hawkins had a white cat named Priscilla. She loved that cat more than anything in the world. The cat ate better food than Mrs. Hawkins. Chris ought to know. He shopped for her groceries. He knew ten cents meant a lot to her.

"Chris!" said Veronica. Then she added sweetly, "I didn't even notice you."

"Oh, hi, Veronica," said Chris. Veronica looked him up and down—mostly down because she was so much taller.

"Going to the same old school?" she asked.

"Uh huh," said Chris. Veronica already knew that, he thought.

"Boy, do I feel sorry for you!" Veronica patted her shiny dark hair and then tucked a wisp daintily behind her ear.

When the elevator stopped at the third floor, Veronica reached over and pushed the CLOSE button. Two little kids were standing outside. Their mouths fell open as the elevator door closed in their faces.

"You'll have to wait," Veronica shouted. "This is an emergency."

"Veronica!" Mrs. Hawkins turned around and glared at her. Veronica turned her back on Mrs. Hawkins and giggled. Veronica thought Mrs. Hawkins was a crazy old lady.

Chris noticed that no one else in the elevator said anything. He figured that they were all in such a hurry, they probably didn't care if two little kids were late for the first day of school. Only Mrs. Hawkins cared enough to say, "Veronica!"

As soon as they reached the lobby, Veronica pushed her way out of the elevator. Then she went tearing through the lobby, shouting, "Out of the way! Out of the way! Lady Jane has to go to the bathroom!"

"My, my," said Mrs. Hawkins. "That's an interesting way of putting it."

When Chris got outside, Veronica was standing between two parked cars waiting for Lady Jane to finish her business. (That's what Veronica called it.) Chris tried to pass her while she was still looking down, but Veronica spotted him.

"Chris! Come here quick. I've got something to ask you."

Chris walked over to the curb. He was carrying his lunch box under his arm trying to hide the picture of the rabbits. He was surprised that Veronica had something to ask him; most of the time she only had something to tell him. She never seemed curious about anyone but herself.

"What I wanted to ask you is—well—how many kids do you think will be in your class this year?"

Chris thought it was a strange question.

"Um . . . I don't know . . . I guess the same as last year. Twenty-eight, maybe 27." (Veronica wouldn't be there, of course.)

"How can you stand it?" shrieked Veronica. "At Maxwell Academy we will only have 12 in each class."

"Oh." Chris didn't know what else to say.

"You can learn much more in a small class," Veronica said. "Mummy says so."

"Mummy?" Chris had never heard Veronica call her mother "Mummy" before.

"Yes," Veronica went on. "Mummy says that in a small class you get more indivisible attention."

Chris didn't know what Veronica was talking about. "Indivisible" must have something to do with the Pledge of Allegiance. " . . . one nation . . . indivisible with liberty and justice for all." Chris still couldn't figure it out. He shrugged and started to leave.

"Wait, Chris!" Veronica shouted. "Did I tell you what my mother's friend said about Gulliver?"

Gulliver was Veronica's cat. Chris was quite interested in Gulliver, but not when Veronica talked about him.

"Well," said Veronica. "You won't believe this, but this lady comes to our apartment— she's my mother's friend and she's a world expert on cats. When she saw Gulliver, she said she never saw such a rare cat. She said we should enter Gulliver in a cat show right away. As you know, Gulliver is half-Persian, half-Siamese, half-Angora, and half-Calico . . . "

Veronica always stared right into your eyes when she talked. Chris wanted to get away from her stare and he wanted to get away from her talk about Gulliver. He had heard this story a thousand times in different ways. Veronica was always telling you what a fancy cat Gulliver was.

"By the way," said Veronica. "When are you going to get your cat?" Veronica knew he wanted a cat very badly.

But before Chris could say, "Oh, any day now," Veronica was saying, "Of course it would be impossible to find another cat like Gulliver. The lady said he is the rarest breed she ever saw."

"I've got to go," said Chris.

"Maybe I'll walk with you," said Veronica. "My school doesn't start until next week."

"I've got to run," said Chris. He didn't want to be seen walking with Veronica. Last year a lot of kids had hated Veronica—mainly because she was such a show-off. Chris didn't hate her as much as they did. That was because he had known her for so long. . . .

Veronica had come to every birthday party he had ever had. And, at every birthday party, when time came to open presents, Veronica always had "one just like that at home—only better." It got to be annoying.

"I've got to run," Chris said again.

"We can run too," said Veronica, and she tugged at Lady Jane's leash.

But Chris just couldn't be seen with Veronica today. Not the first day of third grade. He didn't want people to say, "There go Chris and Veronica."

No, Chris wanted to get to school before the bell rang. He wanted to sit on the steps with Peter. Peter was his best friend and he was the funniest kid Chris ever knew. He wanted everyone to say, "There go Chris and Peter."

Chris started to run. He had reached the corner of the next block before he looked back. Veronica was still standing on the curb. She was staring after him.

"Boy, do I feel sorry for you!" she yelled.

Room 312

Peter was waiting for Chris on the school steps. Chris slid down next to him. He couldn't help noticing that Peter had a plain black lunch box—the kind construction workers carry. Chris carefully placed his book bag over his own lunch box.

"Well, this is it," Peter said sadly. "We've had it. We're finished."

"What?" asked Chris.

"Our teacher," groaned Peter. "You won't believe who we have."

"Who?" asked Chris.

"I don't know how to tell you this . . ." said Peter.

"C'mon, Peter."

"Are you ready?"

"Who? Who? Who?" Chris liked it when Peter tried to drive him crazy like this.

Peter leaned over and whispered, "Mrs. Marmelstein."

"Who is she?" Chris had never heard of Mrs. Marmelstein.

"My brother had her," said Peter. "She hasn't taught for eight years."

Chris thought Peter was lucky to have an older brother. And Peter's mother was president of the PTA. That was the reason Peter always knew everything ahead of time.

"What's wrong with her?" asked Chris.

"Hah!" said Peter. "Why do you think they called her Mrs. Marmelscream?"

"She's a screamer?" asked Chris.

"And that's not the worst part . . ."

The bell rang.

"You'll see," said Peter. "Well, here goes." He sighed and stood up. Chris and Peter walked up the steps together. Chris was feeling happy. He had known since the end of second grade that both he and Peter were going to be in Room 312 this year. It didn't really matter to Chris who the teacher was. Chris was also happy to see that Peter hadn't grown too much over the summer.

"Hi, Peter. Hi, Chris." Jennifer smiled at both

of them. Jennifer was taller than Chris, but shorter than Peter. "Do you know who our teacher is going to be?"

Peter hummed the "Funeral March," and Chris pretended to throw up.

The minute they walked into Room 312, Chris knew things were going to be a lot different this year.

Instead of tables with chairs around them, there were desks lined up in neat rows.

"Stop!" called Mrs. Marmelstein. "Stop right where you are." Chris didn't think she sounded very friendly—not like Mrs. Poster, their second-grade teacher.

Peter froze with one foot in the air. Chris knew he was being funny, but Mrs. Marmelstein didn't seem to get the joke.

"Everyone line up over there," she said pointing to the side wall. "Line up in size order," she called as more children crept into the classroom, staring first at the desks and then at the new teacher.

Chris hated to line up in size order. He knew he would have to be first in line. Just the same, he started out by finding a place in the middle of the line. Then, one by one, every kid in front of him turned around, looked down at him, and moved aside to let him get ahead. Each time he moved up one, Chris got a sinking feeling in his stomach.

Mrs. Marmelstein was over at the windows trying to pull the shades halfway down.

Peter wasn't in line yet. He was walking up and down holding his lunch box like a machine gun. "OK, you guys," he whispered. "Up against the wall or I'll blast you." A few kids giggled.

Mrs. Marmelstein turned around. Peter quickly found his place in the line.

"Class!" Mrs. Marmelstein had a very shrill voice. "Let us not forget we are third graders. We are no longer second graders." She clapped her hands loudly—so loudly that Chris jumped.

"Third graders, I want your complete and undivided attention. I want everybody looking this way." Mrs. Marmelstein took a deep breath. "I want 48 eyes looking straight at me."

Chris didn't understand what Mrs. Marmelstein meant, but he quickly figured it out. After all, math was his best subject. There were 24 kids in the class with two eyes each.

Only 24 kids! He would have to remember to tell Veronica that.

When Mrs. Marmelstein was sure there were 48 eyes looking straight at her, she went on:

"We will be behaving differently from now on. We will not be behaving like second graders any more. Third graders do not run or push. Second graders may run and scream in the halls. Second graders may wiggle around in their seats. But we are not second graders any more—are we class?"

No one said anything. There was a lot of shuffling and whispering. Mrs. Marmelstein went over to the desk and filled in her seating chart.

Chris had to sit at the desk in the front row by the window because he was so short. He cheered up a little when Peter was given the seat right in back of him. But Mrs. Marmelstein was back on her favorite subject—the difference between second graders and third graders.

The class was getting fidgety. There was the sound of desks scraping along the floor. Every few minutes Peter sighed—very loudly. Mrs. Marmelstein was writing a list on the blackboard—a list of terrible things second graders did and the good things third graders were supposed to do. Chris had never even thought of doing most of the bad things second graders were supposed to do.

For instance, Mrs. Marmelstein wrote, "PUTTING THINGS OTHER THAN PENCILS IN THE PENCIL SHARPENER." Chris was trying to guess what kids could have stuffed into pencil sharpeners when Mrs. Marmelstein rapped on her desk. She said sharply,

"All right class, I want 48 eyes looking directly at me."

Jennifer was sitting next to Chris. Chris noticed that she was trying very hard not to laugh. Her hand was clamped tightly over her mouth and her face was bright red. She kept peeking over her shoulder at Peter.

Chris turned around to see what was going on. Peter was sitting back in his seat, his hands folded neatly on his desk. One eye was staring politely at Mrs. Marmelstein. The other eye was tightly closed.

Chris burst out laughing. It was the funniest

thing he had ever seen. Mrs. Marmelstein was only getting 47 eyes!

Suddenly Mrs. Marmelstein was standing over him. Her voice was so shrill, Chris ducked his head. "Let me know when you're finished, young man," she said. "We can wait."

Red Readers, Blue Readers, and Golden Retrievers

Mrs. Marmelstein began nodding her head up and down and looking around at the class. "You see, third graders, this is exactly what I mean by second-grade behavior. I want you all to look at a little boy who is unable to control himself."

Chris stopped laughing. He tried to sit up taller in his seat. Why did she have to call him "little boy"? And why did she have to say that stuff about being unable to control himself? Didn't that mean wetting your pants?

Everyone was quiet. Chris watched Mrs. Marmelstein erase the blackboard. If he started to cry, he would really be acting like a second grader.

"Sorry, Chris," Peter whispered. Chris nodded without turning around. He felt a little better.

"Now," said Mrs. Marmelstein when she had finished erasing the board. "We will be taking a little test so that we can divide you into your reading groups." She handed a stack of papers to Jennifer to hand out.

"There will be three reading groups. Group One—the Red Group—will be for our advanced readers. Group Two—the Yellow Group—will be our good readers, and Group Three—the Blue Group—will be our average readers."

Chris looked down at the reading test Jennifer had put on his desk. There were five pages of purple mimeographed sheets. The printing was so light, it was very hard to read them.

"Absolute silence," said Mrs. Marmelstein. "You have one hour."

Chris thought it was dumb to take a reading test. Everyone always ended up in the same group they were in the year before. He had always been a Yellow Reader—ever since first grade. But in first grade, the Yellow Readers had been called Canaries. (The Red Readers had been Robins and the Blue Readers Blue Jays.)

Chris had never minded being in the Yellow Reading Group. Peter had always been a Yellow Reader too. But it didn't mean "good" reader as Mrs. Marmelstein had said. It meant just plain average reader. And everyone knew the Blue Readers were the worst readers—the dumbest kids in the class.

Chris looked over at Jennifer who was already hard at work. She would be in Group One. She had always been a Red Reader. Chris looked at his chewed-up pencil, and then at the clock.

He tried to concentrate on the first little story in the reading test, but the purple print was so light, some of the words hadn't come out at all. The story seemed to be about a conversation between a fish and a worm. They seemed to be making smart remarks to each other, but Chris had trouble reading the punch line.

After the story came the dumb questions: "Who is smarter—Freddie Fish or Willie Worm?" Chris looked back at the story. It made him angry that the questions never seemed to have anything to do with the story. He thought they both must be pretty smart if they could talk. Finally he filled in "Fish" because he figured that fish had bigger brains.

There were more boring stories. Chris just wanted to get it over with. He was feeling hungry. At lunchtime he would have to remember to tell Peter about the flying armored tank he had seen in the window of Tony's Toy Store . . .

"I saw it too," said Peter when they were sitting in the cafeteria. "It's really cool! Did you see the ad for it on television?"

Chris shook his head. "Is it really on television?" Toys always seemed more glamorous when there was an ad for them on TV.

Chris bit into his peanut butter sandwich. His lunch box with the bathing beauty rabbits was hidden on his lap.

"Want to take a look at it on Saturday?" asked Peter.

Chris nodded happily. Chris and Peter often spent Saturdays at Tony's Toy Store. The owner's name was Nick, and he let the two boys look around for hours if they wanted to. Peter sometimes bought a car or truck. He got a bigger allowance than Chris, but he never bought anything without asking Chris for his opinion.

"You were sure right about Mrs. Marmelscream," said Chris.

"Puh-lease," said Peter. "I'm trying to eat."

After lunch they lined up in size order for assembly. It was a long assembly, and when they got back to Room 312 Mrs. Marmelstein had finished marking their tests. She was busy pinning little red, yellow, and blue circles on the bulletin board. Each circle had a name on it.

The desks had been re-arranged into little clusters. One desk in each group had a sign on it. One sign said RED SETTERS and there was a picture of a beautiful red dog on it. Another sign said GOLDEN RETRIEVERS and the third one said KERRY BLUE TERRIERS. Chris knew it was kind of babyish, but he was pleased to think he was going to be a GOLDEN RETRIEVER this year.

He found a yellow circle with his name on it. Then he went over to a desk in the Golden Retriever group. He moved the desk next to him a little closer. He wanted to save it for Peter.

Mrs. Marmelstein handed him a book called *Fun Around the City*. There were pictures of skyscrapers on the cover. It looked pretty interesting.

"Is this desk taken?" asked Sharon.

Chris nodded and looked around. Why was Peter taking so long?

But Peter was still at the bulletin board looking for his name.

"Over here!" called Chris in a loud whisper. If Peter didn't hurry up, someone would take his seat.

Peter turned around, but he didn't look at Chris. He shrugged his shoulders. Then he went over to the Red Group and sat down at the desk next to Jennifer.

"No, no, no!" called Chris. He looked around. Everyone was staring at him.

But something was terribly wrong. How could Peter make such a mistake! Quickly, Chris got up and went over to the bulletin board. There was a circle that said PETER F. on it, but it was red! Chris's heart began to beat very fast.

"In your seat!" called Mrs. Marmelstein.

Chris didn't even want to look at his reader. He kept peeking over at Peter trying to see what the advanced book was called. All he could see was a red cover with black writing. Chris opened his own reader. It didn't look very interesting any more. He turned to the first page. The page began to blur before his eyes.

He closed the book and looked over again at the Red Setters. Their desks were near the windows and the afternoon sunlight flickered on the wood and metal desks. Suddenly the light seemed so bright, Chris's eyes hurt. He looked away.

At the end of the day, the desks had to be put back in neat rows. All the kids had to pack up their books. Chris turned around and stared at the Red Reader on Peter's desk. Peter was standing next to his desk talking to Jennifer. Chris could read the title. It said, *More Fun Around the City*.

Carefully he opened up Peter's reader to page one to see if he could read that too.

"Hey, what are you doing?" Peter turned around and stared at Chris.

"Just looking," said Chris. He turned to another page.

"I don't think you're supposed to do that," said Peter.

"Huh?" said Chris.

"Well, you see . . . " Now Peter seemed a little embarrassed. " . . . I don't think it's good for you to read ahead. I don't think Mrs. Marmelstein wants you to. That's the only reason I'm saying that."

"Oh." Chris closed the book gently. He picked up his lunch box and his book bag and left Room 312.

Home from School

When Chris got home, he stood in the front hall for a few minutes. There was a big lump in his throat from trying not to cry.

His parents were talking quietly in the living room. He didn't want them to see him. He didn't want them to ask, "And how was school?" He was afraid he would start to cry.

Chris went into the kitchen. Everything had been put away. There were no brown bottles on the counter. The stove and refrigerator were sparkling clean.

"Is that you, dear?" his mother called. Chris didn't answer.

"We're in here," she said.

"I just have to put my things away," said Chris, and he walked quickly down the hall to his own room. All he wanted to do was to close the door behind him, lie down on his bed, and cry.

But he could hardly get in the door to his room. He had left it a terrible mess. Toys and books were all over the floor. And his mother's laundry basket was standing right in the middle of the floor. Dirty clothes were scattered all around. It looked as if his mother had stopped in the middle of collecting the laundry. Chris felt worried.

"Mom!" he called.

"In the living room," she called back.

Chris went to the living room. He stopped at the door and stared. The living room was very neat. There were bunches of fresh flowers in vases. His parents were sitting on the couch drinking tea. On a table in front of them was a large tray of delicious-looking pastries.

His parents looked so happy. How could they be so happy when Chris had just had such a miserable day?

"Sit down." His mother patted the couch next to her.

"Have an eclair." His father sounded so jolly.

"But don't drop it on the couch," his mother added, smiling at him.

"What's going on?" asked Chris.

He squeezed in between his mother and father. They both hugged him.

"I know!" Chris shouted. "You got the check from Orpex!"

"Yup," his father said.

"Oh boy!" said Chris. "Are we rich?"

His mother laughed. "Of course not. We owe most of it. But we are celebrating anyway. We can worry later. And guess what. Your father got a big job for the weekend after next."

"A photograph for a magazine ad," his father said.

"Wow!" said Chris.

"Why does everything good happen at once?" His mother sighed happily. "And how was school?"

"Horrible," said Chris. He picked up an eclair and tried to eat it without spilling any whipped cream. It was very squishy.

"Why horrible?" his mother asked.

"We have to sit in rows," said Chris.

"We always sat in rows," his mother said.

"In the olden days?" asked Chris. His mother gave him a playful punch.

"Yes, dear," his mother said. "We had to sit

in rows and name every capital of every state in the United States."

"Yeah, but there were only 13 of them then," said Chris. "Get it?"

"We get it," his father said. His mother and father were both laughing.

Chris ate another eclair. He felt happy and cozy. Mrs. Marmelstein, Peter, and Room 312 seemed very far away.

After the pastries were all eaten up, Chris asked his mother if she would like to hear some up-to-date jokes. But she said she would be too tired to understand them anyway. And she was much too tired to finish the laundry. So Chris and his mother played a game of Paper, Scissors, Rock.

"Once, twice, three . . . shoot." Chris put out a fist and his mother put out two fingers.

"Hah!" said Chris. "Rock breaks scissors." He rubbed his hands together and then blew on two fingers. Then he slapped his mother's wrist very hard.

"Ouch!" she said. "I'll get you for that. Once, twice, three . . . hah! Scissors cuts paper." And she hit Chris's wrist very hard.

Chris liked playing games with his mother.

She always played to win—not like some grown-ups who went easy on you just because you were a little kid.

Then his mother and father tickled him.

"Help! Help! Help!" screamed Chris.

All at once his mother stopped tickling him and looked at her wristwatch. "Ooops, I forgot. I've got to take you to Dr. Lowe. I made an appointment for a check-up for you at 5:15. We've got to hurry."

"Oh no!" wailed Chris. The fun was over. "She's going to give me a shot! Oh, please Mommy, can't we change the appointment to next week?"

"Find your shoes," his mother said.

They had to take two buses to get to Dr. Lowe's office. Chris spent the whole time thinking about the shot he was going to get. It was better than thinking about Room 312 and Mrs. Marmelstein.

When they got off the second bus, Chris stopped to tie his shoelaces.

"Let's go, Chris." His mother was getting impatient.

They passed an old warehouse and a building

that was being torn down. Chris looked around. The neighborhood didn't look familiar.

His mother took his hand and dragged him up the steps of a strange building that looked like an old hospital. Garbage was lying around on the sidewalk.

"Hey," said Chris, "where are we?"

His mother turned around and looked at him in surprise. "Oh, didn't I tell you? Dr. Lowe moved her office. The rent was too high."

"Oh great," thought Chris. Now he was really depressed. The lobby of the building was dingy and it smelled funny. He was sure a shot in the arm would hurt twice as much in this place. There wasn't any red carpet on the floor as there had been at Dr. Lowe's old office. And there were no fancy toys to play with.

Chris saw a sign next to an old elevator which said, "CLINIC—SECOND FLOOR." So he waited by the elevator while his mother spoke to a lady at the Information Desk.

His mother came and took his hand. They did not go up in the elevator. Instead she led him to a big heavy door at the end of the hall.

They went into a room full of cages.

It was very noisy in this room. Chris covered his ears.

Then he realized that the noise came from the cages. There were dogs barking all over the place.

A girl in a green and white uniform met them. She led Chris and his mother to some cages in a corner. She opened up one cage and took out a tiny striped kitten.

"It's the youngest one we have," she said to Chris's mother. "Seven weeks old, we think."

The girl put the kitten on Chris's shoulder. Chris grabbed it tightly. The kitten sniffed his mouth.

"He's a kisser," the girl said. She was smiling at Chris.

Chris looked up at his mother. She was looking down at him with the happiest look Chris had ever seen on her face.

"Where's Dr. Lowe?" Chris asked.

His mother started laughing. She was laughing so hard, some of the dogs stopped barking. Chris looked around. He suddenly realized he was not at the doctor's office; he wasn't getting a shot; and the kitten he was holding belonged to him.

Domestic Cat

Chris waited while his mother filled out forms and paid for the kitten. The girl in the green and white uniform told them they would have to bring the kitten back for shots on Saturday. Then she gave them a little booklet, "How to Care for Your Cat."

Chris noticed a big chart on the wall. It was a chart with pictures of different kinds of cats. To his surprise there was a cat that looked just like his kitten, but much bigger. It had white paws, but the rest of him was stripes—black stripes, gray stripes—even brown stripes. "DOMESTIC SHORT HAIR," it said. Chris felt very proud. His cat was a Domestic Cat.

Now the girl was putting the kitten in a cardboard box. "Wait," shouted Chris. "Can't I carry him?"

The girl explained that the kitten was better off in the box. Until the kitten got its distemper shot, it should not go outside and it shouldn't be around other animals. "He might catch something," the girl said.

The kitten was mewing loudly. Chris noticed a lady waiting for an appointment. She had a cat, but her cat was in a special carrying case. The case had a window all around the top and the cat could look out. Chris looked back at the cardboard box.

"Mom! Mom!" he whispered. "Can't we get a case like that?"

His mother looked around at the lady with the cat in the case. For a moment she looked unsure of herself.

"Do you sell cases like that?" she asked the girl.

"Yes, we do. They cost $12.95."

"Oh," said Chris's mother in a small voice.

"Please, Mommy, please . . ." Chris begged. He wanted the very best for his kitten.

"I'm sorry, Chris . . ." Then Chris saw that sad look come over his mother's face.

"No, no," he said. "It doesn't matter."

But the look on his mother's face didn't go away quickly enough.

Chris and his mother talked to the kitten all the way home on the bus. They stuck their fingers in the holes of the cardboard box and wiggled them. But the kitten cried the whole time.

"We're almost there," Chris's mother told the kitten. "This is Seventy-second Street. The traffic is bad this time of day." But the kitten mewed even louder. It seemed like a very long ride.

"Hey, Chris." Veronica was in the lobby trying to walk on stilts. She jumped off the stilts and ran over to Chris, dragging her stilts behind her.

"Did everyone ask where I was?" she asked eagerly. Chris stared at Veronica. It took him a few seconds to realize she was talking about school.

"Did they miss me? What did you tell them? Did you tell them I was going to private school?"

Then Veronica noticed the box. She let go of her stilts and they clattered to the floor.

"What's in there?" she demanded.

"I got a kitten," said Chris. "Just now. I got a kitten."

"You did?" Veronica began jumping up and down. Chris was surprised that Veronica should be so happy for *him*. "Can I see it? Can I see it?"

"We can't let him out of the box," said Chris. "He hasn't got his distemper shot yet."

"Where'd you get him?" asked Veronica.

"At the Animal Shelter," said Chris.

"The Animal Shelter? Oh no!" Veronica stopped jumping up and down. "How *could* you? How *could* you get an animal at that place?"

Chris didn't say anything. Veronica looked down at the box and said, "Can I see him anyway?"

Chris shook his head.

"What kind is he?" asked Veronica.

Just then a small paw reached out of the box through one of the holes. The paw began feeling around and clutching at the cardboard with its claws.

"Oh look!" shrieked Veronica. She bent down to pet the paw. The paw tried to grab her fingers. Veronica stood up again.

"Oh please let me come upstairs with you."

Chris shook his head. He didn't want Veronica around on the kitten's first night home.

Chris's mother called him. She was holding the elevator door open for him. "Be right there," said Chris.

When he turned back, he saw that Veronica had opened the cardboard box and stuck her head in. "Oh look!" she squealed. Then she pulled her head back with a jerk. She was holding her cheek. "Ouch," she said. There was a little red scratch on her cheek.

Chris was furious with Veronica. He was embarrassed at the same time. He tried to close the cardboard box.

"Christopher Miles," said Veronica in a low, serious voice. "I think you got ripped off."

"What do you mean?" asked Chris. He was trying to wave away Veronica's germs and close the box at the same time.

"I think," said Veronica, "that you got an *alley cat*."

"He's not an alley cat," said Chris.

"Well then what kind of cat is he?" Veronica demanded.

"A Domestic Cat," said Chris.

Veronica was impressed. "Oh," she said, looking down at the box with respect. "I never heard of them. Where do they come from?"

"From India," Chris mumbled. He picked up the box and ran to the elevator. He couldn't understand why Veronica always seemed to spoil everything.

When they walked into the apartment, Chris's father was taping a sign to the kitchen door—the door that also led to his darkroom. The sign said:

> KEEP DOOR CLOSED
> AT ALL TIMES.
>
> NO CATS ALLOWED
> BEYOND THIS POINT.

Chris didn't think it sounded very friendly.

Chris was sorry too that his room was such a mess. But the kitten didn't seem to mind. He was so happy to get out of the box.

The kitten walked around sniffing at the laundry on the floor. He seemed a little unsure of himself. His back legs were so unsteady he fell down a few times. He sniffed at everything, including Chris's shoes. Chris and his mother just sat on the cluttered bed looking at the kitten.

The kitten crouched down and watched the edge of an undershirt that was hanging from the laundry basket. His tiny body quivered. He pounced at the undershirt and fell over backwards. He scurried to his feet and then sat very still blinking his eyes and looking at the undershirt. Then he began licking his paw very fast, as if all he cared about was getting it clean.

"Did you ever see such a beautiful kitten?" Chris asked his father, who was standing at the door.

His father smiled at him. "Well, to tell you the truth, he looks just like any other cat. In fact, I've never seen such a plain cat." He laughed, and Chris's mother gave him a poke. But Chris didn't care; he was sure his father was joking.

The next moment the kitten was acting as if he owned the place. He pranced around the room, his tail held high. He took another swipe at the undershirt.

"Get your camera!" Chris shouted. "Quick, Daddy, hurry!"

"Not right now." His father sighed. "Besides, I don't have the right film in it."

Chris couldn't believe his father didn't want to take a picture of the kitten. Chris was sure his kitten was the cutest kitten in history.

They fed the kitten two teaspoonfuls of cat food on a little plate. The cat food was called Savory Supper. Chris thought it sounded delicious. The kitten sniffed the cat food on the plate. Then he put his front paws right in the middle of the plate and started eating.

"Where are your manners, kitty?" Chris's mother asked. Everyone was laughing. There hadn't been so much laughter in this place for a long time. It sounded nice.

That night the kitten decided to sleep curled up under Chris's chin. Chris tried not to breathe. He tried to hold very still; he didn't want to disturb the kitten. It was hard to go to sleep.

It was also hard for Chris to sleep because he was so busy trying to think up a name for his new kitten.

It had to be a perfect name. It had to be the best name in the whole world . . .

Getting
on Top of Things

When Chris woke up the next morning, he had a name for his kitten. It came to him the minute he opened his eyes.

His mother always said that your best ideas came to you when you were asleep. That was because your mind was relaxed. What she said must be true because Chris knew at once that he had thought up the perfect name.

"Tiger!" he whispered to the kitten who was now curled up asleep on a pile of dirty laundry.

Chris got to work cleaning up his room. It was still too early for school. He wanted to make his room look more grown up. He moved his desk next to the bookcase. Then he cleared off the top of his desk. He picked up a few fat, important books and stood them up on the corner of his desk. He collected his babyish toys and books and put them on a special shelf for Tiger.

Then another idea came to him. He made his bed and pushed it against the wall. He lined up his pillows along the wall so it would look like a couch instead of a bed. Next, he made a bed for Tiger in the corner of his room with some old blankets and a towel. He tried to make Tiger's bed look like a couch too.

Chris was pleased. His room looked just like an office.

At breakfast Chris wanted to talk about Tiger.

"The name just came to me," he told his parents. "Just like that!" He snapped his fingers.

"How nice," his mother said. Then she turned to Chris's father. "If we pay the whole electricity bill now and half the telephone bill, we can pay the rest when you get the money for the ad."

" . . . and he really likes me," Chris said. "He slept right next to my neck and he sniffs my mouth all the time, like he's trying to kiss me."

"Who?" Chris's father was looking at him.

"The kitten! Tiger! He cuddles up right next to me."

"I guess he likes the 98.6," his father said.

"Huh?" asked Chris.

"The 98.6 degrees Fahrenheit," his father explained. "Your body warmth. That's all cats care about."

Chris picked up his book bag and his lunch box. He didn't think that was a very nice thing for his father to say. Besides, he was sure it wasn't true.

When Chris opened the front door, Veronica nearly fell in. She had been waiting for him.

"Chris," she said. "There is something you should know." Then she noticed his lunch box. "What kind of lunch box is that?" she asked.

Chris didn't care what Veronica thought about the lunch box. Or about his kitten. This morning he was above all that.

But as soon as they got into the elevator, Veronica put her arm around Chris's shoulder.

"I think I should break this to you gently," she said in a very loud voice. The elevator was crowded. Everyone was looking at Veronica.

Chris looked around for Mrs. Hawkins, but she wasn't there.

"I looked it up in my *World of Cats* book." Veronica went on. "A domestic cat is exactly the same thing as an alley cat."

Chris tried to pull away from Veronica.

"Boy, do I feel sorry for you," said Veronica.

Chris didn't say anything. Everyone in the elevator seemed to be listening.

The elevator door opened on the sixth floor. The man who always carried a clarinet case and a briefcase to work squeezed into the elevator. He put the briefcase and the clarinet case on the floor between his legs.

"Maybe you can take him back." Veronica's voice sounded very loud. Chris felt his face get red.

"Well, anyway." Veronica seemed to be enjoying all the attention. "Just keep that cat away from Gulliver."

"Why?" Chris was upset. He had been planning to introduce Tiger to Gulliver as soon as Tiger had had his distemper shot. Then Tiger would have another cat to play with—right across the hall. "Why?" he asked again.

"Oh, you know," said Veronica. She patted

her hair and looked at each person in the elevator.

"No, I don't," said Chris. "Why can't Tiger and Gulliver play together?"

Everyone looked at Veronica to see what she was going to say.

Veronica sniffed and tossed her head. "Because of babies, of course."

"But they are both boy cats," said Chris.

Somebody in the elevator giggled.

Veronica looked around angrily. "I know that," she said. "Even so." Veronica didn't look so sure of herself now. "You can never tell."

"Tell what?" asked Chris. He was beginning to enjoy this.

"Never mind," said Veronica. "Look, Christopher Miles, I just don't want an alley cat anywhere near Gulliver. You know, Gulliver is half-Persian, half-Siamese, half-Angora, and half-Calico . . . "

The elevator stopped. The two little children who had been left behind the day before stepped in.

"Wait a minute," said Chris. "Hold everything." There was something wrong with what Veronica was saying. Then it came to him.

"Veronica," he said slowly. "Did you say Gulliver is half-Persian, half-Siamese, half-Angora, and half-Calico?"

Veronica nodded proudly.

"Then," said Chris, "you have two cats!"

People in the elevator began to laugh. Veronica didn't laugh. Neither did Chris—but only because he wanted to keep a straight face. The two little kids thought it was the funniest thing they had ever heard. They were howling with laughter. And the man who lived on the sixth floor reached over and patted Chris on the shoulder.

"I don't get it," said Veronica.

"Don't you see?" Chris asked. "You can't have four *halfs*. Four *halfs* equals two cats—and you said . . . "

"I know what I said," Veronica snapped. Her face was bright red.

When the elevator reached the lobby, everyone got out except Veronica.

"Say hello to Gulliver," Chris called. "Both of him!"

Veronica glared at Chris and pushed the CLOSE button.

The Sharpest Boy in the Class

Chris saw Peter sitting on the school steps. The first thing Chris noticed was that Peter had his Red Reader balanced on his knees. Chris was sure that Peter just wanted everyone to see how smart he was.

But the next thing Chris noticed was that Peter was sitting with Jamie and Eric. Jamie and Eric were both Blue Readers—the worst readers in the class. Chris was surprised. He had been sure that, from now on, Peter would only be talking to Red Readers.

When Peter called his name, Chris went over and sat down with the three of them. He tried to avoid looking at the book on Peter's lap.

"Why didn't you wait for me yesterday?" Peter asked Chris as if nothing had changed.

"Guess what." Chris just had to tell them. "I got a kitten. Yesterday."

"You did?" Peter looked very happy for Chris. Chris wondered if he was just pretending.

"What kind?" asked Eric.

Chris felt himself blushing. He said, as casually as he could, "Oh, you know, just a plain one—a regular one . . . you know, just an ordinary old everyday-type kitten." Chris didn't think Tiger was the least bit ordinary. Why did everyone have to ask him that question?

"Those are my favorite kinds of cats," said Eric.

Chris was very pleased.

"I can't stand those fancy foreign cats," Eric added.

"He looks like a tiger," Chris said.

The three boys were watching Chris, waiting for him to go on.

"Remember Veronica?" asked Chris.

They all groaned.

"Well, I really let her have it this morning."

Chris told them the story of Veronica and her four half-cats. He did a pretty good imitation of

Veronica's voice and patted his hair the way Veronica always did.

When he got to the punch line, Eric and Jamie burst out laughing, but Peter just looked uncomfortable.

"I don't get it," said Peter.

Chris was amazed. The Blue Readers had gotten the joke right away. Maybe Blue Readers weren't all that stupid. He had to explain the whole thing to Peter four times before Peter finally said, "Oh, I guess I see now." Chris waited for Peter to laugh, but, instead, Peter said thoughtfully, "I think I know what she means . . ."

"I know what she *means*," said Chris crossly.

Then Chris told everyone how he had gotten Tiger; how he thought he was going to the doctor. Peter didn't seem to be listening. He seemed to be thinking about something else.

When Chris finished his story, Peter suddenly stuck the Red Reader in Chris's face and said, "You can look at this if you really want to. I don't care."

Chris stared at the book in his face. Up until this moment, he had been feeling pretty clever. He looked at Eric and Jamie. All at once he thought of something very witty to say:

"Oh, may I?" he asked. "Oh, really? Can I really touch it? Huh? Huh? Huh?"

Eric and Jamie started to giggle. Peter pulled the book away.

But Chris couldn't stop. He moved closer to Peter and began bowing and praying to the book the way he had seen some Arabs pray in a desert movie on television.

"Oh, almighty Reader," Chris said, bowing up and down. "I am your most faithful and humble servant . . . "

"Stop it," said Peter.

" . . . I beg you . . . I pray to you, almighty Workbook . . . "

Eric and Jamie were rocking back and forth with laughter. Peter didn't even smile. He shoved *More Fun Around the City* into his book bag.

All morning in class Chris watched Peter. He watched everything Peter did.

Peter was very well-behaved. He didn't crack a single joke.

And every time Mrs. Marmelstein asked a question, Peter raised his hand.

"Very good, Peter," Mrs. Marmelstein kept

saying. "That's absolutely correct, Peter," and "How interesting, Peter."

Chris was sure Mrs. Marmelstein didn't remember anyone else's name. Other kids in the class were getting mad. Chris could feel it. Whenever Peter began to talk, Chris could hear a low, angry buzzing in the room.

Peter was telling Mrs. Marmelstein about the Indians he had seen out West that summer.

"Very interesting, Peter," said Mrs. Marmelstein. "When we get up to Indians, I am sure you will have a lot of interesting things to tell the class."

Chris turned his head sideways. Then he made a funny sound—halfway between a kiss and a slurp. He got a big laugh for that. Mrs. Marmelstein looked around angrily.

For the rest of the morning, whenever Peter raised his hand to say something, Chris made a kissing-slurping sound. The rest of the class really enjoyed it.

Right before lunch, Mrs. Marmelstein caught him making that sound. She couldn't remember his name; she had to look on her seating chart.

"Christopher Miles," she said. "Do you have something you want to share with the class?"

Chris just sat there smiling up at Mrs. Marmelstein. She didn't scare him today.

"Answer me." Mrs. Marmelstein stood in front of Chris's desk. "Do you have something you want to share with all of us? If it's so amusing, I am sure you will want to share."

Chris shook his head. But as soon as Mrs. Marmelstein's back was turned, Chris pretended to pass out candies as if he were sharing them with the class. "One for you," he whispered, " . . . and one for you, and one for you . . . "

In the lunchroom a whole bunch of kids wanted to sit with Chris. Peter sat alone at the next table.

Chris felt nervous. He knew everyone expected him to be funny all during lunch, but the funniest thing he could think of doing was to swallow his milk and make it dribble out of his nose. It was a pretty old trick, and Chris was afraid that someone would *say* it was a pretty old trick. He was even more afraid that he would never be able to be as funny that afternoon as he had been that morning.

At the end of the day, Peter left class

without even looking at him. Chris was worn out from being the short, funny kid in Room 312. Suddenly he felt homesick for his second-grade classroom and for Mrs. Poster. In second grade life had been so simple—and, Peter had been his best friend.

Chris wanted to get home fast.

The Errand

Veronica was in the lobby when Chris walked into his building. She was busy talking to Lady Jane Grey. She pretended not to see Chris.

The poodle rushed over and tried to jump up on Chris.

"No, Lady Jane," Veronica said, and tried to pull the little dog back.

Mrs. Hawkins was sitting on a chair in the lobby, leaning on her cane.

"Oh, Chris," she called. "Could you run to the store for me?"

Chris didn't want to go; he just wanted to get home to Tiger.

"Sure," said Chris. "I just have to let my mother know."

Chris stood outside the front door to his

apartment. He heard thumping noises coming from inside. He turned the key in the lock and peeked in.

His mother was running up and down the hall in her wooden sandals. Chris couldn't figure out what she was up to.

Then he noticed that his mother was trailing a ball of wool behind her as she ran. Tiger was running after her, slipping and sliding—trying to catch the ball of wool.

His mother noticed him. She stopped. She looked embarrassed. "Oh, hi," she said. Tiger caught the ball of wool. He held it in two paws and tried to eat it.

"I don't know what I'm doing," his mother said. "I've been entertaining Tiger all afternoon. And I have so much work to do." She brushed the hair out of her eyes. "You won't believe this, but your father just told me that he will be taking pictures for the magazine ad right here— right in this apartment!"

"How come?" asked Chris.

"I don't know," his mother said. "All I know is that I have to get the whole place in shape by the Saturday after next." She sighed and looked around. "I was thinking of sanding the floors. They look awful."

"What's the ad for?" asked Chris.

"It's a toy ad — a new dollhouse for Christmas. Your father says they're going to bring a rain machine, so it will look like it's raining outside."

"Wow!" Chris was excited.

"We'll get paid extra for letting them use our apartment." His mother was smiling.

Chris remembered Mrs. Hawkins.

"Can I go to the store for Mrs. Hawkins?"

"Of course." His mother was playing with the kitten again.

"And, Mom," said Chris. "Do you think I could have my week-before-last allowance?"

"Sure," said his mother. She got her pocketbook and took 75 cents out of her change purse. Then she looked down at the kitten chewing on the string. She pulled a dollar bill out of her purse and gave that to Chris too. "Get Tiger a treat," she said.

Chris knew his mother must be feeling rich. She never just handed him a dollar like that.

Mrs. Hawkins was tapping her cane on the floor. She looked worried. But when she saw Chris, she smiled. "Oh thank you, dear," she said. She handed him her shopping list and some money.

It made Chris sad to see the way Mrs. Hawkins handled money. Her money was all bunched up in a small change purse. What made him so sad was the way she looked in the purse after she had given Chris four dollars—she looked again to see what was left.

Chris's mother usually did the same thing. But she hadn't done that today. Chris thought of the way his mother had just sort of tossed him the dollar bill. He felt a little scared. Was his mother throwing money around?

"I might be a few extra minutes," he told Mrs. Hawkins. He would have to go to the pet store to find just the right treat for Tiger.

"Take your time," said Mrs. Hawkins. "I'm not going anywhere."

Chris looked at Mrs. Hawkins' shopping list. It was always the same. She had carefully listed six different kinds of cat food, a 12-ounce box of brown rice, and a package of dried navy beans. Mrs. Hawkins only ate rice and beans. Chris hoped she was getting enough protein and vitamins.

When he was finished at the supermarket, Chris ran to the pet store on the next block.

The bell over the door rang as he walked in. Chris had spent a lot of time in that pet store. But, today, for the first time, he had a reason for being there.

"May I help you, sonny?" The man behind the counter recognized Chris. Chris knew the man was being polite because Chris usually mumbled, "Just looking."

But today he said, "Do you have any special treats for kittens?"

The man showed him where to look. Chris wanted to tell him about his kitten, but he was afraid the man would ask him where he got the kitten. The pet store sold kittens, but only the pedigreed kind. Some of them cost over a hundred dollars.

Chris looked along the shelf. He saw some packages of dried tidbits which were called HAPPY KITTY TREATS; Chris didn't think they looked very tasty. Then he saw a small toy—a tiny bedroom slipper with a bell on the toe. It only cost 49 cents. Chris thought Tiger would enjoy that slipper very much.

He got the slipper and then decided to get some HAPPY KITTY TREATS after all. Each package cost 25 cents so he got two.

As Chris was handing the man the dollar, he suddenly remembered the tax.

"That's OK, sonny. You can pay me later." The man smiled at Chris. "Did you get a cat?" he asked. Chris nodded.

"That's terrific!" the man said. "Good luck with your pet."

Chris left the pet store feeling good. He was glad the man never asked, "What kind?"

On the way home Chris made up his mind to give one bag of HAPPY KITTY TREATS to Priscilla, Mrs. Hawkins' cat, even though she was already very spoiled.

As he was passing the parking garage in the building across the street from his, Chris suddenly stopped. He knew there was a family of stray cats who lived in that garage.

Just then he saw one of those cats picking through a garbage pail. It was a scrawny, dirty white cat with gray spots. The cat stopped what it was doing and looked cross-eyed at Chris.

Chris suddenly felt very strange, standing there with a shopping bag full of cat food and another bag of goodies for Tiger and Priscilla.

"They need it more," thought Chris. He opened Priscilla's bag of HAPPY KITTY TREATS and placed it next to the garbage pail.

Another little gray cat came over and sniffed at the bag. "That poor cat," Chris thought. "It never knows where its next meal is coming from." Chris tried not to feel sorry for it. "After all," he told himself, "these cats are not complaining."

Chris watched the cats for a few minutes. He decided that one day he would bring Tiger here so Tiger could see how tough city cats got along—cats who had no one to take care of them. He began to think that these cats might be happier than the cats who lived with people. "They have each other," he told himself.

Then he wondered if he was just trying to make himself feel better.

Chris walked the rest of the way home thinking about all the poor, brave little cats who have to struggle to make it in this world.

"I hope Tiger doesn't grow up to be a sissy," Chris thought.

That night Chris tied Tiger's new toy slipper to a string and dangled it in front of the kitten. He tried to make it hard for Tiger to catch it. He held it very high.

Chris was proud. He was sure Tiger would not grow up to be a sissy. He held the slipper even higher. This time Tiger jumped up and fell over on his back.

Chris got worried. He was afraid Tiger was hurt. After all, Tiger was only a kitten. Chris decided to wait and train Tiger to be a tough cat when Tiger was a little bigger.

"Have you any homework?" his mother kept asking him.

"Just a little. Just a little."

When Tiger finally fell asleep on the armchair in Chris's room, Chris decided to get his homework over with. All he had to do was to read the first chapter in his Yellow Reader. He didn't really feel like it.

The first chapter wasn't even a real story. It was just a few paragraphs about a boy whose best friend was his book. Chris closed the book. It was so babyish.

Then he tried to think of funny things to do and say in Room 312 the next day. After all, he had a reputation to live up to.

Professor Pete

The next day Chris got fewer and fewer laughs whenever he made the kissing-slurping noise, so he gave that up and started calling Peter "Professor Pete" behind his back. A few kids really liked that.

When Mrs. Marmelstein called the reading groups together—"Red Setters," (clap, clap) "Golden Retrievers," (clap, clap) "Kerry Blues," Chris growled and barked. He was sure Mrs. Marmelstein heard him, but she didn't say anything. "She's ignoring me," thought Chris. "It's just one of those teacher tricks."

Chris never sat alone in the lunchroom that week. Kids crowded around him—even some fourth graders—because all the action was at his table. The action was mostly telling jokes, giggling, and throwing food.

Chris came home every day very tired. He

spent the rest of each afternoon curled up with Tiger—listening to Tiger breathe.

His parents were very busy. His father had a small photography job for a hardware company. His mother spent every day sanding the floor with sandpaper.

"Why don't we rent a machine?" Chris's father asked her.

"I don't like machines," she said.

On Friday morning Mrs. Marmelstein picked Chris to clear all the papers off the bulletin board. Chris was surprised. He looked up from the drawing he was working on. It was a picture of Mrs. Marmelstein with big ears and a trunk like an elephant. (Chris had been doing a lot of funny drawings lately.)

Chris got up and went to the bulletin board. This time Chris was sure it was a teacher trick. Teachers often picked the worst kid in a class to do something. That way, the teacher figured, the kid might feel proud and he might start behaving better.

Chris reached up to pull off a thumbtack. He heard a voice in the class call out:

"Are you sure you can reach, little boy?"

Chris was stunned. It was Peter's voice. And the whole class was laughing.

"That's enough, Peter," said Mrs. Marmelstein.

Chris was quiet in class for the rest of the day. At lunchtime he threw a few carrots around—but it wasn't that much fun anymore.

When school was out for the day, Chris walked slowly down the school steps. He was thinking so much, he almost didn't see Peter, who was sitting on the bottom step.

"Hey, Chris," said Peter quietly.

Chris went over and sat down next to Peter. He thought he ought to apologize to Peter for making fun of him all week.

But Peter said, "I don't have enough money for the flying tank, but I was wondering about that car with the jet engine—you know, the one that goes under water."

"I'm not sure about that one," said Chris. He sat down next to Peter. "I don't think that periscope goes up and down."

"You're kidding," said Peter. "What a rip-off. Um . . . you wanna go and look?"

"Sure," said Chris.

They walked together to Tony's Toy Store. Chris noticed that Peter was still carrying his Red Reader outside his school bag. But Peter's school bag did look pretty full. Chris still wished that Peter would carry his math book outside instead. They all had the same math book.

The periscope did not go up and down.

"Boy, am I glad you warned me about that," said Peter. Chris felt good.

They spent a long time at Tony's Toy Store. Chris hoped his mother wasn't going to be worried about him.

Chris noticed a plain black lunch box—one just like Peter's. It cost eight dollars. He wondered if he should ask his mother to buy it—especially since she seemed to be feeling so rich.

He told Peter about the magazine ad his father was going to photograph right in their apartment.

"You're kidding." Peter was impressed. He was just sorry it wasn't going to be an ad for some electronic game, instead of a dollhouse.

"It's not even for this Christmas," Chris told

him. "It's for next Christmas. You see, advertising agencies have to plan very far ahead. They're bringing a machine to make rain."

"You're kidding," Peter said.

Chris was surprised to see how carelessly Peter was treating his Red Reader. One time Peter just dumped it on the floor while he looked at a toy helicopter on a low shelf.

Peter finally decided to buy a small gasoline truck. The truck didn't do anything special. "But I really need one of those," Peter said.

They both stood at the counter while Peter dug into his pocket to find his money.

As they were walking out the door, Chris noticed that the Red Reader was still lying on the counter.

All the way home, Chris kept waiting for Peter to remember the book, but Peter was too busy talking about his plans for the gasoline truck. "It'll need its own garage," he said.

Chris was getting worried that someone would come along and steal the Red Reader. He had to tell Peter.

But something kept stopping him. And he

was so sure Peter would remember.

When they got to the corner of Chris's block, Peter said, "Bye, see you Monday."

"Bye," Chris said. He was still meaning to tell Peter about the book. But, all at once, it was too late. Peter was gone.

In the Darkroom

That night Chris's father invited him to sit in the darkroom while he printed his photographs of hardware equipment.

Chris loved the darkroom—the sound of running water—the yellow-orange light—the photographs coming up on blank paper like magic. It was so peaceful.

Chris was glad to sit with his father. He had been lying around all afternoon and evening worrying about Peter's Red Reader. But, after all, he told himself, that was Peter's problem.

Chris watched his father put a photograph in a tray with a liquid called *fixer* in it. They had to leave the photo in the fixer for 20 seconds before they could turn on the overhead light to see how it came out.

"Mississippi one . . . Mississippi two . . . "

said Chris. His job was to stand by the switch for the overhead light. When he had counted off 20 seconds, he had to say, *"Ready to go light. Have you checked your paper?"*

Then his father would make sure that no box of photographic paper was open. If a box was open when the light went on, the paper would be ruined. That was because photographic paper was special. It had silver in it. That also made it very expensive.

Once when Chris was two years old, he had pushed open the door to the darkroom. The light from the kitchen had spoiled a whole box of photographic paper. It was really his father's fault; he had forgotten to lock the darkroom door. But Chris still didn't like hearing that story; he didn't even remember doing it.

His father always hummed in the darkroom. Sometimes he played the radio; he said country music helped him to relax. But the job he was doing tonight was so easy, he didn't even put on the radio. All the negatives had come out well, he said, and he didn't have to do anything special when he printed them.

Then Chris's father started talking about the ad he was going to photograph next weekend. He said he was very nervous about the job.

"There will be a million people here," he told Chris. "Wait until you see—the art director from the agency, a make-up lady, the man who will run the rain machine. I'm even going to have an assistant."

His father took photographs out of the fixer and put them in a big tray to wash. He seemed to be enjoying Chris's company.

"But, you know, Chris, I'm not sure about the little girls who are supposed to be playing with the dollhouse. The older one seems OK, but her little sister looks a little too cute. Know what I mean?"

"You met them?" Chris asked.

"Yup," his father said. "I had to help choose the models. Believe it or not, their names are Tiffany and Bambi."

A girl named Tiffany? A girl named Bambi? Chris thought their names sounded so glamorous.

"Yup, Tiffany and Bambi Mervish," his father said. "The mother's coming too. She looks like a real pain in the neck."

Chris sighed. "I'll bet Tiffany is the older one."

"I believe you're right," his father said. "She is exactly the same age as you."

Chris hoped Tiffany wasn't going to be too tall. He felt nervous. He would have a lot to do before next Saturday.

For one thing, he would have to go to the library and take out a lot of up-to-date joke books. He would have to get ready for Tiffany just in case he got a chance to talk to her.

But the joke books made him remember Peter's Red Reader. All at once Chris felt terrible.

"Um . . . Dad . . . " he said. "There is something I was meaning to ask you. Um . . . do you think that if you notice something and don't tell someone you noticed it, it's the same thing as telling a lie?"

"What?" His father didn't get it.

"I mean . . . let's say you see someone—and this someone forgets something that you saw him forget and you know he forgot it and you meant to say something, but you thought . . . "

"Chris!" His father laughed. "I don't get it. Can't you tell me exactly what you mean?"

But Chris didn't want to tell his father exactly what he meant.

Besides, he thought he knew the answer anyway.

Saturday

When Chris woke up Saturday morning, he remembered that today was the day they took Tiger for his distemper shot.

Chris noticed a note taped on his door. It was in his mother's handwriting. Chris thought he'd better feed Tiger. Then he would come back and read the note.

He pushed open the door and stepped out. There was a funny smell in the hall. And his feet were sticking to the floor. "Maybe I'd better read the note," he thought.

He went back into his room.

The note said, "STAY IN ROOM—DO NOT STEP ON WET VARNISH."

Chris peeked out again. The floors looked beautiful. He hoped his parents wouldn't notice the little smudge near his door. Then he heard meowing.

Tiger had gotten out.

Chris closed the door. He thought fast. What if Tiger were stuck to the floor?

"Tiger!" Chris called softly. "Please come back." He didn't want to wake his parents.

Tiger was meowing loudly. Chris couldn't even tell where the sound was coming from.

Then he got an idea. There were some old newspapers stacked up next to his easel. He figured if he laid the newspapers on the floor first, he wouldn't be stepping on the varnish. Since he didn't know how far away Tiger was, he took a whole pile of newspapers.

One by one, he tore off a sheet and placed it carefully down on the floor before he stepped on it. By the time he reached Tiger, he felt quite clever. Tiger was sitting by the kitchen door licking his paws. Chris was glad Tiger wasn't stuck to the floor.

Chris picked up Tiger and carried him back across the newspapers to his room.

Then he tried to rub the varnish off Tiger's paws with a tissue. He didn't think it was good for Tiger to lick varnish.

It was only then that Chris noticed a tray on his desk. His mother had left a bowl of cat food for Tiger and some cereal for Chris. Chris began to wonder how long it takes varnish to dry.

He had been thinking of calling Peter this morning. If Peter hadn't found his book yet, Chris would say, "Oh, maybe you left it at Tony's."

That would be almost as good as telling the truth.

Chris got dressed. Tiger followed him around. Then he and Tiger ate breakfast.

Chris decided to spend the time trying to read his Yellow Reader. He sat down at his desk and opened the book. Tiger climbed onto his lap. Then Tiger jumped up on the desk and walked right across the page Chris was trying to read. Tiger stared at Chris for a very long time. Chris stared back. Tiger blinked first.

Suddenly Chris heard his mother wail, "Oh no!" Chris couldn't figure out what was wrong. Then she wailed again—even louder, *"Oh no! my floors!"*

Chris peeked out and then shut his door quickly. His mother was screaming now, *"There are newspapers stuck to my floors! Oh, Chris, how could you do such a thing?"*

"That was the dumbest thing you ever did," his father told him. He was trying to soak off some of the newspapers with a sponge. It was a big job.

"It would have been better if you had just walked on the floor," his father said.

"Yes, but the note said . . . "

His father wasn't listening. He was scrubbing hard. "We'll have to do them over," he said. "They'll never look as good again."

good night, Chris wanted to hide under the covers.

His father laughed when he saw the kitten draped across Chris's shoulders with his paws resting on Chris's head.

"Tiger looks as if *he* owned *you*," his father said.

"His name's not Tiger anymore," said Chris, trying not to look at his father. "His name is His Royal Majesty Bengal." Even that didn't sound fancy enough.

"I'll never be able to remember that one," his father said. And he began stroking the kitten.

Chris was surprised. "You like him?" he asked his father.

"He's all right," his father said.

"Do you think he's special?" asked Chris.

"Not special . . . no . . . " His father gave Chris a funny look. "Just nice."

"The nicest cat in the world?" asked Chris.

"I'm not crazy about cats in general, but Tiger's not bad—for a cat."

Getting Ready

On Monday morning Peter's book turned up. Someone had found it at Tony's Toy Store and left it in the school office.

"Oh boy!" Chris kept saying. "That's great!" Peter couldn't understand why Chris was so happy. Chris seemed to be even happier than Peter was about the whole thing.

Chris had fun that week. Every day he and Peter sat in the lunchroom together telling jokes. Chris had taken some joke books out of the library and he wanted to try them out on Peter to see if they were good enough for Tiffany. Peter knew some jokes too.

"What about this one, Chris. You say to her, 'Did you hear the one about the airplane?' and she says, 'No,' and you say, 'Oh well, it's over your head.' Get it?"

"Good one," said Chris, writing it down.

On Friday night Chris watched as his father set up lights in the living room. It was very exciting. There were large lights hanging all over the ceiling.

His father placed a small light on the floor next to a table.

"What's that one for?" asked Chris.

"To light up what's-her-name's hair. You know, the smaller one."

"Bambi," said Chris. He felt as if he already knew these two girls who were coming.

"And the dollhouse will be on this table. Her sister will be sitting there. This light will also help separate them from the background."

"Oh," said Chris.

His father put another small light way back next to his camera.

"What's that one for?" asked Chris.

"To give them sparkles in their eyes," his father said.

Some of the lights had gauze over them, attached with clothes pins.

"Why do you have that?" asked Chris.

"To spread the light a little. To make it look softer."

"Oh," said Chris. He had never seen so many lights. "Why don't you just use a flash?" Chris had seen people use flashguns on their cameras. It looked so simple.

"Good question," his father said. "Well, there are lights—big lights like these—that flash. But you can't use them when you want to show rain on a window. They go off too fast. It would make the rain look like it's frozen in mid-air. You would see each tiny raindrop. I want to take a slower picture so the rain looks the same way it looks to the human eye."

Chris thought of another good question. "What if it really does rain tomorrow?"

"No good," his father said. "Fake rain shows up better."

Chris thought his father was very smart.

A man came late that night to deliver the rain machine—a bunch of pipes, some hose, and a big tank.

Veronica was standing in the doorway watching.

"What's going on?" Veronica was in her bathrobe.

Chris hadn't seen Veronica since she started her new school. He knew she was still angry at him because of the four half-cats.

When Chris told her about the ad his father was going to photograph, Veronica got very friendly. And when she heard about the two girls who were going to pose for the photograph, she grabbed Chris's arm.

"A girl named Tiffany? A girl named Bambi? Oh, Chris, can I watch? Oh, please can I watch?"

Chris went to ask his father, who was still busy with the lights.

"Veronica?" his father groaned. "That's about the last thing I need."

Chris went back to Veronica, who was still waiting at the door.

"My father says he would really like to have you come, but the advertising agency won't allow it."

Veronica was very disappointed.

A Girl Named Tiffany

On the morning of the big day, Chris's mother was so nervous she kept burning toast. The apartment looked beautiful, but it smelled of burnt toast. A few windows had to be opened.

Tiger was shut up in Chris's room for the day. Chris was a little worried that Tiger's feelings might be hurt, but he was too excited to think much about it.

The doorbell started ringing at 8 o'clock. Chris's job was to answer the door and ask people if they wanted a cup of coffee.

The first person to arrive was the assistant photographer, a young man named Jimmy. Jimmy had long blond hair and was wearing jeans and cowboy boots. Chris thought he looked like a rock star. "Hi!" Jimmy said to Chris.

Then came the art director from the advertising agency. He had a red beard and a moustache. He was wearing a checkered suit with a vest. He smiled at Chris. "A cup of coffee is just what I need. How did you know?"

Next there was a lady in a pants suit standing at the door. She had a silk scarf tied around her head. "I'm Nancy. I'm the stylist. Are the two girls here yet?"

"Not yet," said Chris. "Would you like a cup of coffee?"

Every time he answered the door, he could see Veronica peeking out of her door. She was watching the parade of people.

Two men came to the door at once. One was carrying the dollhouse, which he set up on the table in the living room. It was a nice dollhouse—white with blue shutters on the windows and a red roof. The other man began installing the rain machine outside the window.

They both thanked Chris for offering them coffee, but said they had brought their own.

Jimmy was unscrewing the camera from the tripod. He loaded it with film and then screwed it back on. Then he loaded an extra camera. Chris watched everything that Jimmy did.

When the doorbell rang the next time, Chris knew it had to be Tiffany and Bambi. His heart skipped a beat. But when he opened the door, there was only one little girl standing outside.

"My mother's parking the car," she said. The girl had long brown pigtails and little bangs.

"Are you Bambi?" Chris felt very shy.

"No," she said. "I'm Tiffany."

"But Tiffany's the older one," said Chris. "I mean—"

"I'm short," said Tiffany cheerfully. "I'm eight. Bambi's only five."

Chris stared down at the girl. She was at least four inches shorter than he was.

"Would you like some coffee?" he asked. Then he blushed.

Tiffany giggled. Chris pretended that he had only been kidding. "Black or with sugar?" he asked. Tiffany giggled again. "I'm Chris," said Chris. "I live here."

By now Veronica was hanging out of her door looking Tiffany up and down.

The elevator door opened. A lady with an even smaller girl stepped out. The lady was carrying a pile of clothes in cellophane bags over her arm.

"In here?" she asked.

"Hi!" said the little girl. She had long pigtails too. "I'm Bambi." She stood on her tiptoes twirling her pigtails around her fingers. Chris looked down at her. His father was right. She *did* seem a little too cute.

"Hi, Bambi," said Chris. "Would you like some coffee?"

Bambi twitched her nose. "What for?" she asked.

Chris's mother greeted Mrs. Mervish and the two girls. "I'll show you where the girls can change," she said, and she led them to her bedroom. Chris went back to the living room to watch them set up.

All the big lights were on. Chris had to blink a few times before his eyes could get used to them.

"Too much reflection on the roof," Chris's father called out to Jimmy. Jimmy dug into a big canvas bag and pulled out a spray can. He sprayed the roof of the dollhouse. It didn't look so shiny anymore.

The rain machine was the most exciting thing Chris had ever seen. The long pipes with little holes had been attached to the outside of the window way at the top. There was a big tank at the bottom. The big tank caught the rain and then pumped it back up through a hose to the pipes. Showers of water came down.

But when Chris looked out the other window, it was a bright, sunny fall day.

"It's costing us a fortune," the art director said.

But Chris's father didn't like it. "The rain is coming down too straight," he said. "It should slant across the window."

"Can you get that thing to slant?" the art director asked the rain man.

The rain man shook his head. "Well, no—not the way it's built."

"What we need is a wind machine," Chris's father said thoughtfully.

"I've got that big electric fan," Chris's mother suggested.

"Get it, Chris," his father said.

They set up the electric fan in the other window. It did blow the rain a little. Chris thought it looked pretty good.

But his father still wasn't satisfied. "Not enough depth," he said.

He turned to Chris's mother. "Is there any mineral oil in the house?"

"I think so," she said.

"Mineral oil?" The art director stared at Chris's father.

"Yup—and a small paintbrush."

Chris wasn't supposed to talk, but he shouted, "I've got one." And he ran to his room to get the brush sitting on his easel.

When Chris got back the rain machine was off. The rain man was sitting on the floor leaning against a bookcase.

Then everyone watched as Chris's father painted slanting streaks of rain across the window with mineral oil.

"I don't believe it," the art director said. "That machine is costing us a fortune."

"It's an old trick," said Chris's father. "But it will look better."

And it did look good. It looked as if there was a heavy rainstorm outside. Even the art director agreed that it looked better than the rain machine.

Tiffany and Bambi came into the living room and sat at the table on either side of the dollhouse. They both held very still while the lady named Nancy arranged their clothes and fixed their pigtails to look just right.

Then Chris's father and Jimmy held exposure meters in front of each girl to see how much light was hitting different parts of their faces. Everything seemed to take forever.

Chris's father was looking at the red sweater Bambi was wearing. He turned to Mrs. Mervish, who was sitting in a chair in the corner.

"Mrs. Mervish, do you have any other clothes for. . . uh . . . "

"Bambi," Chris whispered.

"Don't you like what she's wearing?" Mrs. Mervish looked hurt. "They told me it was an ad for Christmas. I though it looked kind of Christmasy."

"The photo will be in black and white," Chris's father explained. "The other one's outfit is fine." Tiffany was wearing a light blue sweater and a tan skirt.

"Black and white?" Mrs. Mervish looked as if

she had never heard of such a thing. "Well, no one told me," she said.

Chris thought his father was being too fussy.

"The red sweater will come out black in a black and white photograph," his father explained to Mrs. Mervish.

"Why didn't you say so?" said Mrs. Mervish. "I have plenty of other things for her." She took Bambi back to the bedroom. Nancy the stylist went too.

Chris was proud of his father. Maybe you just couldn't be *too* fussy.

They all waited for Bambi to change. All at once the rain man sneezed. He sneezed again. "There's a cat in here," he said. "I'm allergic to cats."

Then Chris saw Tiger. Tiger was playing with a light cord. Tiffany saw him too.

"Oh, what an adorable kitten," she said.

Chris's father was busy talking to Jimmy. He hadn't noticed Tiger.

Tiger went and rubbed against the art director's legs. The art director looked down.

Quickly Chris reached over and grabbed Tiger. He put Tiger back in his room. "Please be good," he begged Tiger.

"All taken care of?" the art director asked

when Chris got back. He smiled at Chris as if they shared a secret. Chris liked him very much.

Bambi came in wearing a frilly blue blouse and a flowered skirt. She twirled around for everyone to see.

"I guess it will do," said Chris's father.

Mrs. Mervish looked hurt again, but she sat down quietly in her chair.

They were ready to begin shooting.

Tiffany was very good. She played with the dollhouse with a peaceful, happy look on her face.

But Bambi had a cute, surprised look on her face. It was almost as if someone had painted it on her like a doll.

"Um . . . Tiffany, that's nice," Chris's father called. "But . . . um . . . what's-her-name . . . "

"Bambi," said Chris.

"Right, Bambi. Bambi, could you try to look a little less surprised?"

When it was time for lunch, Chris sat on the floor next to Jimmy. Tiffany sat next to him, but she didn't say anything to him and he didn't say anything to her.

They ate enormous sandwiches that came from a deli. Then everyone went back to work.

Chris's father was still having trouble.

"Er . . . Tiffany . . . could you lean a little bit toward your sister and um . . . *you* . . . " (he pointed to Bambi) " . . . could you swing around a little in your chair?"

Bambi did what he told her to do, but she still had that cute, surprised expression on her face. Chris knew his father was getting discouraged.

"Yes . . . Tiffany, that's fine," he said. "But . . . um . . . Dumbo, could you look a little more interested in the dollhouse?"

Dumbo? Chris looked at his father to see if he was trying to be funny, but his father looked very serious. He was still talking.

"I'll tell you what, Dumbo. Why don't you play around with the furniture in the living room of the dollhouse."

Chris had to say something. "Daddy," he said in a loud whisper. "It's not Dumbo; it's *Bambi*!"

"Oh, yeah." His father looked embarrassed. "I knew it was from some Disney movie."

Now Bambi was really surprised. "He called

me Dumbo!" Then she wrinkled up her face and tried to cry. "That man called me Dumbo!" she wailed.

"He just made a little mistake," her mother told her. "Now just do what the nice photographer wants you to do."

But Bambi was tired. She started to cry—for real. "I don't even like this dollhouse. I like my one at home better."

Nancy had to fix Bambi's make-up all over again.

Chris left the room. The whole thing was making him nervous. When he got back he saw his father talking to the art director. And, to his surprise, Bambi was playing with the dollhouse.

"I can't get this bathtub up the stairs," she said to Tiffany. "It won't fit."

"Why do you want to do that?" asked Tiffany.

"I just do," said Bambi.

"OK," Tiffany sighed. "I'll help you."

For a few minutes they both looked very happy. They seemed to be enjoying the dollhouse. Chris thought it looked like a very cozy rainy day scene.

But his father wasn't paying attention; he was still talking to the art director. He had his back turned to the two little girls.

The camera was still pointing at the girls. It was on its tripod. Then Chris noticed that, although his father didn't seem to be looking, he was snapping pictures very fast.

"Wow!" thought Chris.

Suddenly the big lights blew out. Only the little ones were on, but his father went right on taking pictures.

Bambi and Tiffany finally looked up to see what was happening.

Chris's father turned to Chris and said, "Chris, will you show Jimmy where the fuse box is?"

"Sure," said Chris.

"Time for a break," his father called. "Time for a break, everybody."

The Break

"Please show me your kitten," Tiffany whispered to Chris during the break. She was supposed to be sitting quietly in Chris's parents' bedroom with her mother and her little sister.

"OK," said Chris. "Sure."

He pushed open the door to his room. Tiger was asleep on his armchair.

"Oh," said Tiffany. "He's beautiful. Can I pick him up?"

"Sure," said Chris. "Just call him Tiger."

"Hi, Tiger," said Tiffany softly. She picked him up very gently and carried him around in her arms. She walked around the room looking at Chris's toys. "He's lovely," she said.

Tiger was purring.

Chris wondered if now was a good time to start telling Tiffany jokes.

"I have the same reading book," she said, pointing to *Fun Around the City*, which was lying on Chris's desk.

"In third grade?" asked Chris.

"Yup," said Tiffany. "Did you read the story about the girl and the valentine?"

"I was just about to read it," said Chris.

"I really liked it," said Tiffany, and she carefully put Tiger down again in the armchair.

Chris was sure it was going to be a good story if Tiffany thought so.

Chris was feeling good about everything until Bambi pushed open the door to his room.

"Ooh," said Bambi. Her eyes opened wide. Tiger was sitting on the armchair giving himself a good bath. He was licking himself all over.

"Yuck," said Bambi. "Why is he licking himself *there*? Yuck."

Chris wished Tiger would stop doing that. He tried not to look at Tiffany until he heard her say, "Don't be silly, Bambi. All cats do that."

Then Bambi went over to Tiger and grabbed him by his neck. She tried to pick him up by his neck and his tail.

"No, Bambi," screamed Tiffany. "You'll hurt him." She took Tiger away from Bambi and held him close.

Bambi stood in front of Tiffany.

"Mommy," she yelled.

"What is it, dear?" called Mrs. Mervish from the other bedroom.

"Tiffany won't share."

"Share, Tiffany," called Mrs. Mervish.

Bambi reached over and tried to pull Tiger away from Tiffany. She was squeezing Tiger's stomach very hard.

"Don't do that," said Chris as politely as he could. Bambi let go.

"Mommy," she screamed. "They won't let me have a turn. It's my turn."

"Let her have a turn," called Mrs. Mervish. She sounded very tired.

But Chris and Tiffany wouldn't let Bambi anywhere near Tiger.

A few minutes later, Mrs. Mervish appeared in the doorway. "My goodness, Tiffany," she said. "Put that dirty animal down."

"He's not dirty," said Tiffany, but she let him go. "He's so nice," she whispered to Chris. "I wish I had a kitten just like Tiger."

Chris was sorry when it was time for Tiffany to leave. He thought she was the nicest girl he had ever met.

"Bye, Chris." Tiffany smiled at him. They were all standing in the hall.

Veronica was in the hall too. She was holding Gulliver in one arm and Lady Jane Grey in the other.

"I go to Maxwell Academy," Veronica announced. Everyone turned to look at her. "Where do you go to school?"

"We go to the Professional Children's School," said Tiffany politely.

Veronica's mouth fell open. She just stared as they all got into the elevator.

Chris's father developed the film right away. He was very nervous. He wanted to see what his negatives were going to look like.

"A few good ones," he told Chris. "Want to see?"

The negatives were hanging to dry in the darkroom. There were 10 strips hanging from wire hangers attached to a clothesline. His father had taken 200 pictures!

His father pointed to the last strip.

"That's the only good roll. When Bambi was trying to get that bathtub up the stairs—before the fuses blew."

But Chris didn't want to get too close. He was afraid to even breathe around those negatives.

Tiger

Chris stayed in bed Sunday morning thinking about all the excitement of the day before. He thought about Tiffany and he thought about how he might like to be a photographer when he grew up. "If I get paid every week," he told himself.

The apartment was quiet. His parents were sleeping late. Chris thought about Tiger. He hoped Tiger wasn't going to turn into an unfriendly cat because of the way Bambi had treated him.

Chris got out of bed. He went to find Tiger. But Tiger wasn't in the usual places. Tiger wasn't curled up in the rocking chair in the living room. He wasn't in the laundry basket. He wasn't playing around with the leaky faucet in the bathtub.

Tiger couldn't be in his parents' room. They always shut their door tight so that Tiger wouldn't come in and pounce on their feet. He was only allowed to do that when they were reading in bed.

Chris checked under his own bed again. He went back to the bathroom and pulled back the shower curtain. Sometimes Tiger got tangled up in it.

Then Chris noticed that the bathroom window was open. He suddenly felt dizzy. What if Tiger had fallen out? What if Tiger had tried to jump into the bathtub and had fallen out the window?

Chris went to the window and tried to see if there was a dead cat lying on the sidewalk below. The street was quiet; it was Sunday morning. Chris closed the window and got dressed in a hurry. He found his keys and went out the door, down the elevator, and onto the sidewalk.

He ran around the building to look on the sidewalk under the bathroom window. No Tiger.

Chris went upstairs again. Tiger had to be somewhere in the apartment. As soon as he walked in the front door, he saw that the door to the kitchen was open. He looked in all the kitchen cabinets, but he didn't find Tiger.

The door to the darkroom was open too.

Chris's heart started pounding. He went into the darkroom and turned on the light.

He didn't see Tiger. He saw negatives piled in a heap on the floor. They were all tangled up. Chris bent down. The negatives were a mess. There were teeth marks in some of them.

He heard a noise behind him. He turned around and saw his father standing in the doorway in his pajamas. His father was looking sleepily at Chris.

Then Chris's father saw the negatives. His face turned purple.

"What the . . . "

Chris stood up and stared stupidly at his father. "I just went wild, I guess," said Chris.

Then they both heard a noise. There were boxes of photographic paper stacked up on a table. The pile of boxes was waving back and forth. Then one box toppled over and hit the floor. Paper scattered all over the place.

Tiger leaped out from behind the boxes and streaked through the door past Chris's father.

Chris watched as his father threw away all the damaged paper and put the negatives in a tray of water.

"Are they ruined?" Chris kept asking.

His father didn't say anything.

"Will they be all right?" asked Chris.

"The teeth marks are only in the good ones." His father's voice was breaking. Chris had never heard his father cry. His father's hands were shaking too.

"Can you fix them?" asked Chris.

"Get out of here, Chris," his father said. "Just leave me alone."

Chris ran to his room. Tiger was on his desk, chewing on his Yellow Reader. He swatted Tiger off the desk. Tiger yelped.

"Bad cat! Terrible cat!" Chris screamed.

Then he threw himself on his bed and began to cry. He was crying without making any noise. It hurt to cry that way.

The Plan

Hours went by. Tiger came and curled up next to Chris. Chris didn't yell at Tiger anymore. He knew this was the end of Tiger. He knew they would have to bring Tiger back to the Animal Shelter. Chris wanted to enjoy Tiger's company while he still could.

His mother knocked on his door. Chris quickly pulled the covers up to hide Tiger.

His mother's eyes were all red. She looked terrible. All she said was, "Time for breakfast."

"I'm not hungry," said Chris.

"I don't care if you're hungry or not." His mother left the room, slamming the door behind her.

Chris didn't move. What if another family got Tiger—a family with a little girl in it like Bambi—the type of girl who squeezed kittens?

"No," he said. And he sat up. He would have

to give Tiger to someone he trusted.

The first person he thought of was Veronica. But then he remembered how much Veronica hated alley cats.

Peter! Chris got up and went into his parents' bedroom. There was a telephone next to their bed. He shut the door and dialed Peter's number.

"Hello?" Peter's mother sounded as if the telephone had woken her up.

"Can I please talk to Peter?"

Peter got on the phone. "Hi, Chris."

"Peter," whispered Chris. "I can't talk long, but do you need a cat?"

"What?"

Chris explained what happened as quickly as he could. "We'll have to take him back to the Animal Shelter."

"My mother's allergic," said Peter. He sounded upset. "Chris, you *can't* take him back. Do you know what will happen if you take him back?"

"No," said Chris.

"They'll put him to sleep," said Peter.

"Huh?" Chris thought of Tiger, who was already asleep on his bed.

"Put him to sleep. Put him to sleep." Peter

sounded alarmed. "Don't you get it? That's the nice way of saying, 'Kill him! Gas him . . . ' "

Chris didn't let Peter finish. He hung up the phone. He knew what he had to do.

His mother was in the kitchen putting plates of hot pancakes and sausage on the table.

"I think everyone needs a little cheering up," she said. "I made a nice breakfast."

She went to the darkroom door and knocked. "Dear, you have to eat breakfast sometime," she called to Chris's father.

Chris waited until his mother wasn't looking. Then he grabbed five cans of cat food and the can opener.

He took them back to his room and put the cat food and the can opener into the fancy carrying case. He picked up Tiger and put him in the case too.

"Now, Tiger," he whispered. "They are very nice cats. You'll like them. And they can teach you lots of things."

The carrying case was heavy. Chris tiptoed to the front door and out into the hall. He pushed the elevator button and waited.

"I'll visit you every day," he told Tiger. He looked at the five cans of cat food. That should be enough to last him until he learned to pick through the garbage like the other cats.

The elevator door opened. Mrs. Hawkins was inside. She was dressed for church.

"Hello, dear." Mrs. Hawkins smiled at him. "What have you got there?"

Mrs. Hawkins! Why hadn't he thought of her? Chris would be very happy if Tiger lived with her.

"Mrs. Hawkins," said Chris as he stepped into the elevator. "Could you use an extra cat?"

Mrs. Hawkins laughed. "Me? I have enough trouble with Priscilla. Besides, Priscilla doesn't get along with other cats."

Chris tried to hide the case behind his back.

"What have you got there?" asked Mrs. Hawkins. "My, what a beautiful kitten. You're not trying to get rid of that kitten, are you?"

Chris shook his head. He was so choked up he couldn't talk.

"I hope you named him Tiger," said Mrs. Hawkins.

When they reached the lobby, Mrs. Hawkins hobbled out.

Chris walked slowly out the front door. When

Mrs. Hawkins turned at the corner and waved good-bye, Chris ran.

He ran to the parking garage where the stray cats lived. They were out on the sidewalk. After all, it was Sunday morning and the garbage cans were full of Saturday night party garbage.

Chris put the carrying case down. Tiger was crouched on the bottom.

Chris quickly opened the cans of cat food and lined them up against the wall of the building. "That should last Tiger five days," he thought. He stood back. "By then Tiger will be able to get his own food."

Slowly he lifted Tiger out of the case and placed him gently on the sidewalk. Tiger crouched low. He was breathing very fast. The other cats were watching him.

"I'll say he ran away," thought Chris, and he backed away farther. "No one will ever know."

The kitten looked so small in the middle of the sidewalk. Tiger began to cry. His tiny mouth looked like the biggest part of him as he wailed loudly.

Then Chris saw the other cats sniffing the

five cans of food. In a few seconds more cats joined them and all the food was gone.

"Go away!" screamed Chris. Tears were streaming down his face.

He ran back and scooped up Tiger.

He had forgotten to take his keys. He had to ring the doorbell.

"Chris!" His mother looked frantic.

"I tried to get rid of him," Chris sobbed. "I tried."

Chris's father came out into the hallway. He looked worried. "Where were you, Chris?"

"I was going to free Tiger," said Chris. "I was going to stick him back in the alley where he belongs."

"Oh, Chris." His mother hugged him. "It wasn't his fault. It was my fault. I was the one who left the kitchen door open." And she began to cry.

Chris's father looked from one to the other.

"Stop all this howling," he said. "Let's eat breakfast!"

Back to Normal

When they were all seated around the breakfast table, Chris suddenly felt very hungry. His mother asked him if he wanted his pancakes and sausage heated up, but Chris shook his head. They didn't taste bad cold.

"How is it going?" Chris's mother asked his father.

"One negative isn't too bad," his father said. "Funnily enough, it's one of the ones when the lights blew out." He looked at Chris. "Want to take a look?" he asked.

Chris went into the darkroom, and his father pulled a print out of the wash basin. He held it up for Chris to see. Bambi looked nice; so did Tiffany. But the whole photo was very light and sort of misty. Most of the light was coming in through the window. The rain looked very nice, but the photo wasn't exactly realistic.

Chris liked it. It looked dreamy. His father was watching him.

"Then everything is all right?" asked Chris.

"No, Chris. The job is a disaster. I had to call the art director and tell him what happened. I told him there were only one or two pictures we could use."

"You told him?" asked Chris.

"Of course," his father said. "You see, an advertising agency likes to see all the pictures. They like to choose themselves."

A disaster? Chris felt sick. "What did he say?" he asked his father.

His father laughed. "He just said, 'Well then, we'll make the best of whatever you have.' No one likes to shoot all over again. Besides, the art director wants me to look good because it will make him look good."

Chris looked again at the dreamy photo of a rainy afternoon. "I think he'll like this one."

"Who knows," his father said.

"I *know* they'll like it," said Chris. "It's the most beautiful photograph I ever saw." He hugged his father's arm.

They were sitting again at the breakfast table when the doorbell rang. His mother went to get it.

"It's Veronica, Chris," she said when she came back. "She wants to see you."

"Oh no," said Chris. "Not her. Can't you tell her I'm not home?"

His mother shook her head.

"Well, say I'm busy. I do have a lot of homework."

His mother sighed, and went out again.

Then she came back. "Oh, Chris," she whispered. "Veronica looks so unhappy."

Veronica unhappy? Chris didn't believe that.

"Oh well, let her in," Chris grumbled.

Veronica marched into the kitchen and sat on a stool by the stove. Chris didn't think she looked unhappy at all.

The first thing she said was, "Oh, we had pancakes and sausages for breakfast too—only we had real maple syrup . . . pure maple syrup."

"That's nice," Chris's mother said.

"Fresh from Vermont," said Veronica.

When Chris finished eating, he and Veronica went back to his room. As they were passing the living room, Veronica said, "You still don't have a color TV? How can you stand it? We have two of them."

Veronica hadn't seen his room since he had fixed it up for Tiger. "I liked it better the other way," she said, and sat down on his bed. Tiger climbed up on the bed, but Veronica didn't seem to notice him.

Chris went over to Tiger's shelf and took out his old Tinker Toy set. He sat on the floor and began building a maze for Tiger. He figured he ought to do something useful while Veronica was talking. He couldn't stop her anyway.

Veronica was worse than usual. "And I'm getting a new typewriter," she said. "Lots of kids at Maxwell have their own typewriters."

Tiger crawled onto Veronica's lap, but she still wasn't paying attention to him. She was too busy telling Chris how wonderful Maxwell Academy was—how they had the latest gym equipment—how the stage in the auditorium was so professional, it even had colored spotlights.

Chris didn't even try to talk. He just said, "Uh huh," to everything Veronica said.

Finally he said, "Well, I'm glad you like it so much."

"Did I say that?" Veronica asked. She became quiet. She started to pet Tiger. She was quiet for so long, Chris began to be worried about her.

"Well, don't you like it?" Chris finally asked her.

Veronica laughed in a funny choked up way. "Well, I ought to love it for the money it costs." She stared at Chris. Her eyes seemed clouded over. "Listen, Chris, I'm not allowed to tell anyone, but do you want to know how much my parents are paying for that place?"

Chris shook his head. He really didn't want to know. He felt very tired. He tried to concentrate on the maze. Then he heard Veronica sniff. Chris looked up. Veronica was looking out the window. Her eyes were filled with tears. Chris looked away quickly.

"I hate it!" Veronica started to cry. "I hate it! It's the most h-h-horrible place and . . . n-n-no one likes me."

Chris didn't know what to say.

"They all l-l-look down their noses at me.

They're all a bunch of . . . *snobs*!"

Chris went to close the door. Veronica was making a lot of noise.

"They all have these maids and country houses and things like that and no one invites me over or anything and this girl Kimberly says to me, 'Where do you live?' so I tell her and she says, 'You live there? I thought that was a slum.' "

"What a snob!" Chris said.

"You're telling me?" said Veronica, and she began to cry even harder.

"Don't cry," Chris said.

Tiger seemed to sense something was wrong. He rubbed his head against Veronica and sniffed her mouth.

Veronica stopped crying. "He kisses!" she said. "Look, Chris, your cat kisses!" She sighed. "I wish Gulliver did that."

Chris didn't believe he had heard right. "What did you just say?" He stared at Veronica.

Veronica started talking very fast. "Oh, nothing . . . nothing . . . um . . . all I said was I wish Gulliver could . . . um . . . get a part in a movie. You know, Gulliver is a highly intelligent cat. Did I tell you what a friend of my father's said when he saw Gulliver? He said he wanted to put Gulliver in the movies—and he's a Hollywood producer. He said we should at least let Gulliver try out for a part in a cat food commercial . . . he said . . ."

Veronica was off again. But this time, Chris didn't mind. Suddenly, for no reason at all, he found himself smiling at her.

Veronica stopped talking and looked up at Chris. And, for no reason at all, she smiled back.

115168

DATE DUE   115168

J
R

AUTHOR
Robinson, Nancy K

TITLE
Just plain cat.

DATE DUE	BORROWER'S NAME	ROOM NUMBER

J
R
Robinson, Nancy K
Just plain cat.

Ohio Dominican College Library
1216 Sunbury Road
Columbus, Ohio 43219

DEMCO